SEBASTIAN'S MONSTER

Question Guide

Tanya Popovski

Published by PoP-O Books 2018

www.popobooks.com.au

A catalogue record for this book is available from the National Library of Australia.

Book cover design and formatting services by BookCoverCafe.com

First edition 2018

ISBN 978-0-6482019-4-6 (pbk)

Contents

Getting Started

Kindergarten and year-1 reading expectations are quite different to those of mid to upper primary. In the early years, the focus is on decoding (learning how to read using symbols, sounds, sentences, and visual features). As the reader moves through the grades, the focus of reading in the classroom is about making meaning. The reader is then taught skills to deepen their understanding in order to read to learn.

The chosen book should be at a level below the reader's reading level. If you judge that the text is too difficult for the reader, choose a book at a lower level. This will allow the reader to concentrate on the meaning of the story, thereby encouraging higher-order thinking.

There is no need for pre-reading since a competent reader at this level will be able to read the text. The book should not be read in one sitting. Ask the comprehension questions after the reader has finished the text on each page. Continue to do this for approximately fifteen to twenty minutes. It is acceptable to take more than two sessions to complete questioning of the story. Go at the pace of the reader.

Tips for Using the Question Guide

This symbol ⭐ indicates that an explanation for the word or phrase used can be found in the list at the back of this guide, which you can refer to for further clarification.

This book should not be seen as a text but rather a conversation of learning. When you have asked the reader each comprehension question, give them time to think before responding. The answers have been provided so you can give the reader the answer, which becomes a teachable moment.⭐

If the reader has limited experience with a particular concept, take the opportunity to explore it further through the use of other resources (books, internet, etc). To use **Stop Annoying Me** as an example, if the reader has no understanding of the way a bull behaves, the words 'raging bull' will have no meaning. In this instance, you could take a moment to explain.

The answers provided in the **Question Guide** are general, and are given as examples only of acceptable answers. If the reader's answer is not relevant to the text, or cannot be justified with evidence from the text, this becomes a teachable moment. Give the answer, and show how you worked it out. The reader's responses do not have to cover all of the suggested answers.

If the reader's prediction of the title is not relevant to the clues on the page, avoid correcting their prediction straightaway. Instead, wait until they have finished reading the story to address the initial prediction. For example, you could say: 'At the beginning of the story, you predicted that the title would be [*repeat the reader's initial prediction*]. Now that you've read the story, how accurate do you think your prediction was? What clues could you have used on the title page to help you predict more accurately?'

The superscript numbers at the end of the questions relate to the tracking sheets (purchased separately at www.popobooks.com.au) and are linked to the Australian Curriculum.

Comprehension Strategies

Good learners draw on a range of comprehension strategies to deepen their understanding of written text. The **Question Guide** has been intentionally formulated to use the six comprehension strategies to explicitly teach how we understand texts. They are colour coded, with each colour corresponding to one of the six strategies.

Making connections   Learners make connections with self, text and what is happening in the world.

Predicting   Good readers use the information from illustrations, text and experiences to predict what will be read.

Questioning   Good readers clarify meaning and aim for a deeper level of understanding by posing and answering questions.

Monitoring   Good readers know what to do if something in the text doesn't make sense.

Visualising   Good readers bring text to life by creating mental pictures from what they are reading.

Summarising   Good readers are able to locate the most important ideas in a text and retell them in their own words.

SEBASTIAN'S MONSTER
Tanya Popovski

Title page

Allow the reader to read the title and look at the illustration.

Looking at the front cover, what do you think this story is about?[2]
The reader will respond based on the information on the front cover.
If the reader has made little connection to what is on the cover, the
following question will help to establish that a prediction is not a
guess but a statement based on what the reader knows, and what
they have read or seen.

What information is there on the front cover to support your
prediction?[3]

- The monster and Sebastian are playing together and therefore
  they are friends.
- We can confidently infer that the boy is named Sebastian
  because, other than the monster, he is the only other character.

Why is there an apostrophe before the letter *-s* in the word
Sebastian?[15]

Sebastian's refers to a possessive  .
The monster belongs to Sebastian.

ONE night, Sebastian called out, "Mum, Dad, I can't sleep, there's a monster in my room."

Page Four

Allow the reader to read the text aloud.

➡️ Describe the setting ⭐ of the story.[7]
Sebastian was wearing pyjamas and sitting on his bed with a teddy close by, so we can infer ⭐ that he was in his bedroom at nighttime.

➡️ Looking at the illustration, can you tell how Sebastian was feeling?[7]
Scared, worried

Have you ever felt this way?[1]
Reader to give a personal response.

➡️ Use clues in the text on this page to decide how many people were talking.[15]
There was one person talking, and that was Sebastian.

What is the name of these symbols: " ". Point to the symbols on this page.[15]
They are referred to as speech marks, quotation marks, or inverted commas.

➡️ As a writer, when would you use speech marks?
To indicate that someone is speaking.

What do speech marks tell you to do when you are reading aloud?[15]
They tell you to be expressive by changing your voice to show feeling.

Sebastian's room was filled with toys. Bears, Lego, dinosaurs and toy trucks lined his shelves.

Page Five

Allow the reader to read the text aloud.

 Using the text and the illustration, describe Sebastian's room.[5]
- Lots of toys
- Soft toys, Lego, dinosaurs, trucks, robot, books
- Shelves
- Pet fish
- Bed

In what ways is your room the same as or different from Sebastian's?[1]
Reader to give a personal response.

Thinking about your age and the way your own room looks, use the things in Sebastian's room to guess what age he is and explain why you think this.[9]
He could be six to eight because he has a lot of soft toys and trucks. If he was older, a teenager perhaps, he might not have many toys, and instead he could have a desk with a computer and shelves of textbooks.

Every night, Sebastian's parents came in before sleep time to say goodnight.

Either Mum or Dad read Sebastian a story, gave him a kiss on the cheek and switched off the light as they left the room.

Page Six

Allow the reader to read the text aloud.

What is a routine?[17]
It's a way of doing things in a repetitive way and a particular order.

Sebastian's bedtime sounded like a routine. Which part of the text tells you this?[5]
The text tells you that this happened 'every night'.

How would you describe the sort of a mood the author has created?[11]
The author has created a calm mood.

How does this page connect with what you read at the start of the story on page four?[10]
This is a flashback showing what normally happens at Sebastian's bedtime. It explains what happened before Sebastian cried out for his parents.

Mum came back into the room and asked Sebastian calmly, 'What does this monster look like?'

'Well, I'm not sure. It was dark, and I didn't get to see it clearly.'

'Did it tell you its name?' Mum asked.

'No,' Sebastian said, feeling confused. He was hoping his mum would say there were no such things as monsters.

Page Seven

Allow the reader to read the text aloud.

What was Mum's mood like? Did she seem distressed, and if so how do you know this?[8]

Mum was calm and simply asked Sebastian questions. The text says that Mum questioned Sebastian 'calmly'.

Why do you think Mum was calm?[12]

- She didn't want to add to Sebastian's distress.
- She may have had to calm Sebastian many times before and she was used to it.

Why was Sebastian confused?[12]

Mum began asking questions about what the monster looked liked and if Sebastian knew its name. He hoped his mum would comfort him by saying there were no such things as monsters.

Judging from Mum and Sebastian's reactions, do you think Mum had often questioned Sebastian in this way?[10]

No, because Mum asked about the monster and Sebastian was confused by this.

Why is each part of the conversation written on a new line?[15]

If there are two or more characters in a story, it's important to know who is speaking.

'Does it have little ears?' Mum queried.

'Maybe,' said Sebastian.

'And does it have big feet?'

'I don't know,' said Sebastian.

Page Eight

Allow the reader to read the text aloud.

Why do you think Mum was still trying to find out about the monster?
Reader to make a prediction.

Would you expect your mum to react in the same way as Sebastian's mum if the same thing happened to you?[1]
Reader to give a personal response.

Do you know what the word 'queried' means?[17]
If the answer is no, ask:
Can you infer ⭐ what the word means by using the context (using the clues in the text before and after the word)?
Queried: to question or request information about something

What is the base word ⭐ of queried?
query

What words could you use instead of queried?
Synonyms: questioned, inquired, asked

Why do you think there are so many different illustrations of the monster?[7]
Mum was asking questions about what the monster looked like so there were many possibilities.

Sebastian forgot how scared he'd been.

He was stunned that his mum knew so much about the monster.

Page Nine

Allow the reader to read the text aloud.

Do you know what the word 'stunned' means?[17]
If the answer is no, ask:
Can you infer⭐ what the word means by using the context (using the clues in the text before and after the word)?
Stunned: astonished, shocked

Can you tell me a synonym⭐ for 'stunned'?[16]
Synonyms: amazed, astonished, staggered, astounded

Why did Sebastian forget 'how scared he'd been'?[5]
He was stunned that Mum seemed to know about the monster.

What prediction can you make about what Mum knows?[2]
Reader to make a prediction.

'So, Mum, do you actually believe that I had a monster in my room?' Sebastian asked in a squeaky voice.

'Yes, I do, and I think I might know exactly who is in your room. When I was a little girl, Scooty used to come and wish me goodnight. At first I didn't know why he came, and I was just as scared as you.'

'Who was Scooty?' Sebastian asked.

Page Ten

Allow the reader to read the text aloud.

From this text, how do you think Sebastian was feeling now?[12]
He was a little worried about Mum's answer because his voice squeaked when he asked. A squeaky voice can mean nervousness.

What did Mum reveal?[4]
- The same thing had happened to her when she was little.
- She thought it was the same monster.
- Her monster's name was Scooty.
- Scooty had been friendly, and wished her goodnight.

On the previous page, how accurately did you predict what Mum might know compared with what you now know Mum knows?
Reader to draw a conclusion about how similar or dissimilar their prediction is compared to what Mum does know.

What are the main ideas ⭐ so far?[18]
- Sebastian saw a monster and was scared.
- Mum questioned Sebastian to see if the monster was Scooty.

And so Sebastian's mum told him the story of Scooty.

'When I was your age, I used to hold my doll tightly when I was trying to fall asleep,' Mum said. 'Sometimes I would see a monster in my room. I'd call out to my parents just like you did, but as soon as they came into my room the monster always vanished.'

Page Eleven

Allow the reader to read the text aloud.

How was Mum's experience similar to her son's experience?[5]
- It happened at nighttime in her bedroom.
- She was holding a toy.
- She saw a monster and called for her parents.
- The monster was not there when her parents came into the room.

If you were Sebastian, how would you have been feeling right now?[1]
- A little relieved
- Still confused

Who does the word 'they' refer to in this sentence: 'I'd call out to my parents, just like you did, but as soon as they came into my room the monster always vanished.'[15]
Sebastian's mum's parents.

'My parents used to comfort me and tuck me in, give me a kiss and tell me it was just my imagination,' Mum said.

'What did you do?' Sebastian asked his mum.

'I devised a plan. I started leaving a little pile of biscuits beside my wardrobe. I knew that if the monster started eating them I'd be able to talk to it. It would be too busy munching on the biscuits to munch on me.'

Page Twelve

Allow the reader to read the text aloud.

Is there any part of the text that you're unsure of?
Discuss any parts of the text the reader is unsure of.

Do you know what the word 'devise' means?[17]
If the answer is no, ask:
Can you infer ⭐ what the word means by using the context (using the clues in the text before and after the word)?
Devise: invent, plan

Can you replace 'devise' with a synonym ⭐ ?[16]
Synonyms: think up, design, invent, formulate, concoct, hatch

Do you know what the word 'onomatopoeia' means?
If no: Onomatopoeia is when a word's pronunciation (the way in which the word is said) is like the sound. Examples include bark, chirp, click, growl.

Is there a word in the text that is an onomatopoeia?[4]
munch

What did Mum mean when she said: 'It would be too busy munching on the biscuits to munch on me.'[6]
The monster would be so busy eating the biscuits that there would be no opportunity for it to eat her.

Do you think this plan would work? Justify (provide a reason for) your answer.[13]
Reader to give a personal response.

'The next
night, as soon as
my parents left my room,
I took out the bag of biscuits that
I'd been hiding all day. They were all
crumbly by then, but I didn't worry about
that. I put out the biscuits and crept back into
bed. My room was dark and silent.'

'Were you scared?' Sebastian asked.

'Yes, a little bit,' she said. 'My fear had started
to creep up inside me, but I was determined to
push it away and carry out my plan. I heard
a rustling sound near my wardrobe. I took
out my torch and turned it on. There stood
a giant blue and furry creature. It had tiny
ears on the sides of its round head, and
its feet looked like flippers. It didn't look
that scary at all.'

Page Thirteen

Allow the reader to read the text aloud.

What did Mum do when her parents left her room?[6]

She put out the bag of biscuits and crept back into bed.

How did Mum's feelings change from the beginning of this page to the end?[5]

- She was a little bit scared.
- She was fearful as she waited.
- She was determined to push away her fear.
- When she finally saw the monster, she wasn't as scared as she thought she would be.

The use of adjectives★ helps us to be descriptive. Why is it important, as a writer, to use descriptive language?

Descriptive language creates a mood, person, place, thing, event, emotion, or experience.

There is a lot of descriptive language in this text. Can you find two examples?[4]

- 'My room was dark and silent.'
- 'Fear had started to creep up inside me.'
- 'I heard a rustling sound.'
- 'Giant blue furry creature.'
- 'It had tiny ears on the sides of its round head, and its feet looked like flippers.'

Why is it important to use descriptive language? How does it help you as the reader?[15]

- It helps to paint a picture in your mind about how an object looks, sounds, smells, tastes or feels.
- It's more interesting.
- It gives you insight into what the character is feeling, hearing or seeing.

'The furry creature told me that his name was Scooty,' Mum said, 'and Scooty and I had a long talk together.'

'What did you talk about?' Sebastian asked.

'He told me that it was his job to look after me, and he hadn't meant to scare me. So every night after that, after my parents had said goodnight and turned off the light, I said goodnight to Scooty. I felt safe and secure, knowing that Scooty was there looking after me, and I always slept soundly.'

Page Fourteen

Allow the reader to read the text aloud.

If you were Mum, how would you have felt listening to Scooty's explanation?[14]
Relieved, happy, safe, secure

On the previous page, Scooty was not gender specific (we didn't know if he was a boy or a girl, but now we do). How did the language change to tell us that he was male?[15]
At first the text referred to the monster as 'it' and then it changed to the pronoun ⭐ 'he'.

How do you think Sebastian was feeling or thinking as he listened to the story his mother was telling him?[12]
Amazed, surprised, interested

Would Sebastian be doubtful of the truth of his mum's story?[8]
Probably not, because the same thing was happening to him.

After hearing his mum's story, Sebastian felt a lot calmer and happier.

But he wasn't totally convinced that his mum's monster was the same monster as his monster, so he devised a plan …

Page Fifteen

Allow the reader to read the text aloud.

 Why did Sebastian feel as though he also had to devise a plan?[8]

- He wasn't convinced (he wasn't sure) that his monster was the same as his mum's.
- He may not have believed his mum's story.

What might your plan be?
Reader to give a personal response.

Summarise ⭐ the story.[19]

- Sebastian was scared because of the monster in his room.
- He was surprised his mum knew so much about his monster when she asked him questions.
- Mum told Sebastian that she devised a plan to talk to her monster.
- Mum found out that Scooty was there to keep her safe.
- Sebastian wanted to see for himself if his monster was really Scooty.

Who is the main character in the story?[6]
In the beginning it seemed like Sebastian was the main character, but the story gradually became more about his mum's experiences.

How has the author created mystery and intrigue?[9]
It is a cliffhanger. The unresolved ending leaves a sense of suspense.

What possible reasons could there be for the author to end the story in this way?[9]

The conclusion is left to the reader's imagination.

The author is preparing readers for a sequel⭐.

What do you think readers are meant to be left wondering about?[18]

- Did Sebastian's plan work?
- Did he see his monster?
- Did Sebastian talk to the monster to determine if he was the same monster as the one that visited his mum?

What can you infer⭐ about the illustration of the monster on the title page?[10]

This could be Sebastian's monster, because there was no description of it in the story.

Words and Phrases Used in Chronological Order

teachable moment An unplanned opportunity that arises in the classroom where the teacher has an ideal chance to offer insight to their students; not something that can be planned for; a fleeting opportunity that must be sensed and seized by the teacher. If the reader is unable to answer the question, answers the question incorrectly, or after prompting is still unsure, take the opportunity to tell them the answer and show them how you reached that conclusion.

infer Using clues from the story to figure out something that the author doesn't tell you. Using facts, observations and reasoning to come up with an assumption or conclusion (e.g. *The ground was wet and the leaves were moving around.* Inference: It had been raining and it was windy.) *On Jocelyn's return from her holiday, her plants were limp and droopy.* Inference: Her plants had not been watered during the time that she was away.)

possessive A noun indicating ownership (e.g. *The dog's bed*).

setting The physical surroundings within in a story where and when an event takes place.

base word A part of a word that cannot be broken down, giving it its basic meaning. Sometimes base words have letters added to the beginning and end of the word. A base word can also be referred to as a root word.

	BASE WORD
fastest	fast
magical	magic
luckily	luck

synonym A word or phrase that has exactly or nearly the same meaning as another word or phrase in the same language.

main ideas Teaching readers to know what the main ideas can be difficult. The main idea is the most important part of the story. It helps readers understand the main theme of the story without giving too much detail. Think of *who* and *what* to generate the main ideas.

adjective A word that describes a noun (e.g. *a beautiful boy, a majestic swan*).

pronoun A word that can take the place of a noun or noun phrase that has already been mentioned or is already known (e.g. *I, me, mine, you, yours, his, her, hers, we, they, them*).

summarise Teaching readers to know how to summarise can be difficult. To summarise, the reader needs to extract the essential information from the story with the main idea and details to support the main idea.

sequel A story that is complete in itself but continues from the previous story to create another one.

Learn with